This book belongs to:

....

....

....

For my dear hat-wearing sister, Jessie.

A BRUBAKER, FORD & FRIENDS BOOK,
an imprint of The Templar Company Limited

First published in the UK simultaneously in hardback and paperback
in 2014 by Templar Publishing, Deepdene Lodge,
Deepdene Avenue, Dorking, Surrey, RH5 4AT, UK

www.templarco.co.uk

Copyright © 2014 by Tor Freeman

First edition

ISBN 978-1-84877-358-5 (hardback)
ISBN 978-1-84877-363-9 (paperback)

Printed in China

OLIVE
AND THE
EMBARRASSING
HAT

TOR FREEMAN

B F & F

BRUBAKER, FORD & FRIENDS

AN IMPRINT OF THE TEMPLAR COMPANY LIMITED

Joe had bought Olive a gift.

"They're matching hats!" said Joe. "And they say BEST FRIENDS on them, because that's what we are."

"Oh, yes," said Olive. "Thank you, Joe."

Olive and Joe saw
Ziggy on his skateboard.
"Hi Ziggy!" said Joe.

"Hurrrp!" said Ziggy
when he saw their hats.

"I'm not sure it's quite hat weather today," said Olive.

"Well, it's not really a weather sort of hat," said Joe. "It's more of an everyday hat!"

"I suppose so," said Olive.

Olive and Joe
saw Lola in the park.
"Hi Lola," said Joe.

"Hee, hee!"
said Lola.

"Um," said Olive,
"maybe I should take off
my hat so I don't lose it…
It's a bit big, really."

"Great," said Olive.

"It's okay," said Joe.
"These hats are so stretchy
they won't ever fall off!"

Joe stopped to sniff some flowers.
Matt was nearby, doing a painting.

"Ha, ha!" said Matt.
"Boy, Olive, you do look silly in that hat!"

Olive's stomach was hurting, so she went to sit down.

How lovely and peaceful it was under the tree.

"Olive!" said Molly.
"What HAVE you got
on your head?"

"I'm not Olive," said Olive.

Olive just wanted to be alone.
But then she heard footsteps.
Someone else was coming!

She couldn't bear it any longer.
Olive had to do something.

OLIVE!

"Don't you like your hat?" said Joe.

Joe! oh... I... um...

said Olive.

But it was too late...

Joe had gone. Oh dear.
Olive had NOT been a good friend.

She had to make it up to Joe.

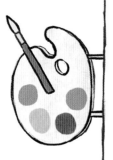

Olive went into the shop on the corner.

Five minutes later she came out again.

She was wearing a sign. It said, "Olive and Joe are best friends."

Olive looked really silly now!

Olive stood on the pavement.

Lola and

Molly and

Ziggy and

Matt

saw Olive.

"Ha, ha, ha!" they said.

"What?" said Olive.

Along came Joe.

"What are you doing, Olive?" he said.

"I am wearing my favourite
hat and my new sign,"
said Olive.

"The sign says:
OLIVE AND JOE
ARE BEST FRIENDS…"

"because that's what we are."